Praise for Storyshares

"One of the brightest innovators and game-changers in the education industry."
— Forbes

"Your success in applying research-validated practices to promote literacy serves as a valuable model for other organizations seeking to create evidence-based literacy programs."
— Library of Congress

"We need powerful social and educational innovation, and Storyshares is breaking new ground. The organization addresses critical problems facing our students and teachers. I am excited about the strategies it brings to the collective work of making sure every student has an equal chance in life."
— Teach For America

"It's the perfect idea. There's really nothing like this. I mean, wow, this will be a wonderful experience for young people."
— Andrea Davis Pinkney,
Executive Director, Scholastic

"Reading for meaning opens opportunities for a lifetime of learning. Providing emerging readers with engaging texts that are designed to offer both challenges and support for each individual will improve their lives for years to come. Storyshares is a wonderful start."
— David Rose, Co-founder of CAST & UDL

Storyshares presents

Storyshares
Storyshares, LLC
24 N. Bryn Mawr Avenue #340
Bryn Mawr, Pennsylvania 19010-3304
www.storyshares.org

Interest Level: High School
Grade Level Equivalent: 3.5

ISBN 9798885978293
Book design by Saskia Globig

the Bollywood Hero

Rachita Ramya

Storyshares

Contents

ONE

I woke up with the hangover of cigarettes and caffeine feeling like smog in my small apartment. I had overslept my nap time. I quickly shut down the alarm clock that had been buzzing for the past hour.

First day of work and you are already screwed! I thought.

The life of a struggling screenwriter in Mumbai was not interesting enough to write about. So I had to grab onto other people's stories, like a parasite.

I got into an autorickshaw on one of the busiest streets in Mumbai.

"Where to?" the driver asked me as he hurried through thick traffic.

"Worli," I said to him. I checked the full address on my phone.

My next big story, or rather the hero of the story, was waiting for me there. The producers of the film had set up an interview with him. It was now up to me to share his story with the rest of the world, hopefully through a good movie.

"We are here, Madam," the driver said. "The meter says one hundred rupees."

I didn't like to bargain. I paid him the last of my money and sighed.

You better do well on this film, Niyati! I thought.

Angry honking from cars made me feel even more tense.

I wasn't used to the different moods of the city yet. This was only my second year of living here. I had a lot of adjusting left to do.

At the end of every month, I had to pay the rent, internet, and electricity bills. I always had a massive nervous breakdown about it. My worries about money made me plan my return trip to the simpler life in Chandigarh.

But in the end, I always ended up staying for some reason.

Maybe this film was supposed to be my reason.

Fighting to live my dreams was harder than I

had thought. I did not give in to my parents' pressure to become a doctor, engineer, or civil servant. I was born a rebel.

First, I took a stand against eating spinach. Then, against Mom chopping off my hair to give me an uneven haircut. And finally, against more important things like career norms.

But enough about me. This story was never meant to be about me.

This story was about a hero. Someone who had saved a hundred lives on an out-of-control train that caught fire. Someone who had risked his life to reach the burning engine and stop the train just in time. Someone who refused to be made into a celebrity. Someone who had stayed anonymous.

Luckily, the filmmakers got the insider information. They knew his name before everyone else did. He was called Vikrant Sahni.

The producers told me he was against being named and famed. He would only work with us if we respected his terms without any arguments.

That is why the producers had sent me here. I came across as a harmless girl who could not negotiate to save her life.

I knocked on the plain-looking door of Vikrant Sahni's apartment.

The smell of fresh onion rolls from someone's kitchen hit me. I heard my empty stomach growl. I had barely scraped through the day with a meal of instant noodles and spiced chai lattes. I was surviving on low-budget, processed, junk food.

In reality, I was broke. The starving kind of broke. Fortunately, I had been hired for my dream job at just the right time. Any later, and I would have been the homeless kind of broke.

Since I was starting out, I wasn't paid the big bucks. I had traded in the stack of money for a strong recommendation letter. I really had to get this script right to be offered more money.

Moved by hunger, I knocked again, a little louder this time.

The door opened. I saw the man behind it.

He was tall. His spine was straight. But as I focused on his face, I noticed it had been badly scarred by the accident.

There were gashes, scars, and burn marks covering a face that had been once handsome. His nose was broken. His silver-rimmed glasses were crooked on top of it.

This was not how I imagined a hero would look.

"Yes?" he asked. His voice was hoarse and deep.

"I am here for the interview, from Traj Film studios," I said.

Vikrant gave a solemn nod and let me in. He stopped me in the hallway suddenly.

"No cameras, no pictures, and no recordings," he said.

"Don't worry, I will treat your house like a museum where all those things are banned," I said.

My joke did not get a very big laugh from him.

"Who is playing me in the movie?" he asked me.

I went all dreamy-eyed.

"Murat Khan," I said.

He was the reason I had agreed to work for the bare minimum wages.

Murat was a creative genius, a magical canvas for showing any character. From perfect comic timing to emotional range, Murat could do it all. To add to his talent, he was blessed with good looks and a stunning smile.

I could not believe I was going to write dialogue for him. Just imagining speaking to him made me starstruck.

Vikrant snapped his fingers to bring me back to the present.

"He does not look like me. He is too... attractive," he said.

"Don't worry, the makeup team will make him look uglier," I said. I bit my tongue.

Like I had pushed some sound button, my stomach growled.

This time he laughed out loud. It was a cool, confident laugh that made him look *attractive*.

"I will get you something to eat," he said.

As he fried some eggs in the kitchen, I got busy looking at his humble home. I could see he lived alone. He also loved dogs but did not own one right now. Maybe he didn't want to replace one he had lost.

From the many pictures on the walls, I could tell he loved traveling. He had been a pilot before this. He was also a nationalist. He could have been a bachelor.

"What are you doing?" Vikrant asked.

He had caught me snooping around in his bedroom.

"I— I was just looking for the story," I stuttered.

"I am here to tell the story, aren't I?" he asked. "You can write your precious script later, *after* interviewing me."

This man was unbelievably rude.

I grabbed the dish of fried eggs he had made for me and pouted.

He tried softening his voice. "Look, you can be a buffer between me and the film people. I will tell you everything that happened on the train from my point of view. You can write it in the script. I just don't want film people bothering me for anything else after this," he said.

"Okay," I agreed.

I had tried to do my own research, but this man was a social media ghost. He also had not given any personal interviews. The producers had heard about his heroic actions from other people. Just him agreeing to talk to me should be a sweet deal.

"Tell me, is it true you weren't even supposed to be on that train?" I asked.

He frowned. "How did you know that?" he asked.

"I read a survivor's story on Facebook. Tell me everything from the beginning," I said.

It was still hard for me to imagine Vikrant as a hero. But Murat Khan could definitely make the story look convincing. He could pull off all the stunts. Through my lens, I was already picturing Murat doing the unbelievable things Vikrant had done.

Vikrant Sahni looked like more of a sidekick to me.

"I had come to say goodbye to my sister at the station. She was leaving for Delhi on another train," Vikrant said. "But suddenly my dog, Mochi, was no longer by my side. I realized he had run off to the next train. That is how I got on board. But before we could both get off again, the train was already at full speed."

"Did you know a group of bandits had planned to hijack it?" I asked.

"No," he said. "As soon as the train passed

the main station, there were a couple of robberies. The men had wrapped their faces in scarves. They had also lit one of the cabins on fire to keep passengers from getting to the engine."

"Where was this fire?" I asked.

"Somewhere in the front cabins. The driver and the railway staff had been captured. The ticket collector was also attacked," Vikrant said. "I tried knocking out one of the bandits. I wrapped my face in his scarf, then sneaked into the engine. I called the control room and helpline numbers."

He went on. "None of the emergency brakes were working and the fire was starting to grow. I tried slowing the train. I told the passengers to use their blankets to smother the fire. The bandits were already out by this time," he said.

Vikrant shook his head. "But the train was still moving fast. We could not get everyone to jump off of it. Finally, we got signals from the base station. The train was stopped at Gorakhpur," he said.

As he told his whole story, I was so caught up in listening to him that I had completely forgotten to write it down. I had to count on my memory, now.

"As I understand, you also helped with taking the hurt passengers to the nearest hospital," I said.

His head gave a tiny jerk of agreement. "Is that all?" he asked.

No, it wasn't. I still needed a hook in the plot.

"I hope you don't mind me asking, but where was your dog during all of this?" I asked. "You did get on the train because of him."

"I had already lost him by then. The fire hadn't been so kind to him," Vikrant said.

"I am sorry," I said.

But even though I was sad about his dog, I had found the perfect hook.

TWO

"And the hero has no character arc or backstory," I said.

I let out a frustrated sigh. Writing a script about a character I had only met once seemed impossible. Even though I was given creative freedom, the inspiration for writing Vikrant's story was hard to find.

I crumpled up the pages and tossed them in the trash can. I needed more inspiration. But before that, I needed caffeine. I could only start fresh afterwards.

"The first thing a writer needs is a good coffee machine. Always invest in a good coffee machine."

My film school teacher's words echoed in my mind. Until I could afford a good one, I had to make do with my French-press plunger. I used it to make a lot of spiced chai lattes.

In the middle of pouring freshly brewed coffee into a cup, my eyes went to my phone. I froze at the message.

Murat Khan wants a reading of the first draft. Make it happen today!

The coffee had already spilled by then. I wasted another ten minutes doing an awkward dance. Murat Khan wanted to meet me!

Nothing mattered more than that. Not even the fact that I was completely unprepared and without a script.

The meeting was in the high-end coffee shop of a luxurious, five-star hotel. I was just hoping the bill would be taken care of, but then Murat Khan's handsome face appeared before me. Suddenly, I was willing to pay whatever it cost to meet him.

"This is Niyati, the writer of our script," the producer said, introducing me.

I felt like I had traveled back in time to become a shy fifteen-year-old girl again.

"Hi, Niyati," Murat greeted me.

My heart fluttered like a butterfly. He was even

more handsome in real life.

The producer interrupted the little moment between Murat and me. "Is the first draft ready?" he asked.

I suddenly noticed that the producer reminded me of a toad. The same beady eyes, the same snout.

"Well?" he asked.

"Err... Yes. But it needs work, it's still very raw," I said.

I had miraculously written a short draft of the plot on my way here. Murat was my muse. Imagining him in every frame made the words flow easily on paper.

"I like the idea of it. It needs more work, but I like your take," Murat said to me, after reading his copy.

I learned my stomach could do somersaults.

"Yes, it needs work. Also, replace the dog with a girl, a love interest. Otherwise, it won't look real on screen," the producer said.

"But it *is* real," I said. "Vikrant got on the train because of the dog."

"Do as I ask," the toad-like producer ordered.

Just as Murat was about to leave, he leaned toward me.

"Niyati, I like to be fully prepared as a character," he whispered. "I'd appreciate it if you could find out more about Vikrant. His mannerisms, his passions, his beliefs, his flaws. Anything that gives my character more depth."

I nodded my head like a schoolgirl.

He added, "After you have written the script, I would also want reading sessions. So the dialogue comes naturally to me."

"Of course, anything you need," I told him.

I did not think I would be back at Vikrant Sahni's house so soon. Murat Khan wanted a good character sketch. I had no other choice but to bother Vikrant.

I knocked again. I wondered why he did not have a doorbell.

The door creaked open. Vikrant stuck his head outside.

"You again," he said.

"I need more understanding of your character," I blurted out before he had even let me in.

"I already told you everything I know," he said.

"Murat Khan wants to act like you. For that, he has to get to know you a little. In this case, through my words," I said.

"Tell him he can play me in any way he likes," Vikrant said.

"But he wants it to be real!" I cried out. "Look,

this is my big break. My career depends on the film's success. I really want to do my best."

He sighed. "Okay, come in," he said.

I quickly went in before he changed his mind.

"What more do you want to know?" he asked.

I looked at him with my writer's eyes. Behind his glasses, his eyes had a hint of vulnerability.

"You wear glasses?" I asked.

"Yes," he said. He looked confused. "That's your big question? You can literally see that I have glasses on."

"But aren't you a pilot?" I asked.

He suddenly looked away. "That was before," he said. "My vision went bad in the middle of my career as a commercial pilot. I had to quit."

"Oh, I see! Do you have nearsightedness?" I asked.

He nodded. "They told me my myopic eyesight could lead to accidents, so I had to leave," he said.

"Is that why you wanted to prevent the train's accident? To feel useful?" I asked.

I hadn't planned on psychoanalyzing him like this. It just happened.

Vikrant looked annoyed at my question. "Look, I understand you want a story, but I just got on the train because of Mochi," he said.

"But you kept helping even when you had lost your dog. Why?" I asked.

"I was still on the train," Vikrant said. "So were a hundred people whose lives were in danger. It was instinctive."

I thought about what he said, but I could not get myself to agree with it.

To act like a hero wasn't instinctive to a lot of people. My first reaction would have been to run and hide instead of walking into an engine blazing with fire.

But I had what I came here to get.

I now had the inspiration for a character.

THREE

"You love me, I know it!" Murat Khan shouted at me.

I felt like his eyes were casting some sort of spell to stop me from leaving.

"I don't love you," I said, after a long pause.

"You do! Why do you want to deny it and waste time?" he asked.

"I am not lying," I said. "I am leaving Mumbai forever to go back home. You should forget me and move on."

Murat looked heartbroken. I almost wondered if I should change my answer to please him.

No, Niyati, don't break character now! I thought.

"But I love you!" he finally said.

I knew this was going to happen from the first day of shooting. But hearing him say those words I had written just made me lose track of everything. I found myself zoning out.

"Umm, Niyati?" Murat said. He looked confused. "We still have the rest of the scene's dialogue left."

"Can we take a break?" I asked. These reading sessions to come up with dialogue were more work than I had expected. "You can practice with Jeanette 'til then."

"But she doesn't even know Hindi!" Murat said.

Jeanette was the actress who had been hired to play the part of Mochi, the love interest. She was actually from Sweden and did not speak a word of our language. It didn't matter. All foreign imports sold like hot buns in India. Drop-dead gorgeous Jeanette was expected to do well against Indian actresses.

"*Je shant manger n'importe quoi,*" Jeanette said. It sounded like she was speaking French.

It did not make sense to me. Jeanette was not even from France. Whether she spoke Swedish or French, dubbing was the movie industry's answer to all language barriers.

We were all inside the film studio. We were just about to shoot the scene where Mochi leaves Vikrant to get on the train.

My thoughts wandered back to the real Vikrant. Over the past six months of film production, I had gotten to know him too well. Being with him felt easy and relaxed, unlike how I felt on a film set.

Murat cut into my thoughts. "Niyati, I have realized you might be a better actress than Jeanette," he said.

I laughed. "You know, I actually came to Mumbai to act, but I guess life had other plans," I said.

"Really?" he asked. "You can still do that! Just exercise a little and eat right. You can look as glamorous as some of these actresses."

I didn't know if that was supposed to be a compliment. Suddenly I felt like there was something wrong with the way I looked.

Was I a little chubby? Did I not dress right?

"Fire! Fire!" someone on the set shouted. I straightened up right away. I was filled with nervousness. The fire scene was supposed to be shot today. I had been hoping nothing tragic would happen on set.

"I need to get out of here," I could hear Murat say to someone. "Can't afford to let anything happen to my face."

"Relax everyone! False alarm!" a man from the production team called, before things got out of control. "It was just a hair dryer that caused a harmless spark. Calm down!"

Out of the corner of my eye, I could see Murat give a sigh of relief.

I thought about what Vikrant had told me about saving people from the fire.

It was instinctive.

Feeling panic at our false alarm on set made me understand

Vikrant's words. It was instinctive. It was instinctive to either act out of cowardice or to act out of courage.

It just depended on who you were. A born hero or a play-acting one.

FOUR

I could finally think about the happiest moment of my life. It was the day of the film's premiere.

After a lot of coffee and cigarettes, all my hard work was finally paying off. I had already bought myself a coffee machine. But if this film was a success, I would buy a newer, better model.

The crowd was going wild, screaming Murat's name at the top of their lungs. I had always known that people in India glorified Bollywood celebrities. I had actually been one of those starstruck people, myself. But now all the screaming sounded a little over the top, even to me. I was done fangirling.

If you ever want to know how it feels to be

God, you should look at life through the eyes of a popular Bollywood actor.

People touched their feet and wrote them emotional letters. They laughed when they laughed. They cried when they cried. They tried all sorts of silly things to get their attention. They even believed their hero could punch twenty men at once to save the heroine.

I used to feel that same way. I used to watch films with fascinated attention, clap when the hero made an entrance, and dance when a Bollywood song played on the radio. But working behind the scenes on an actual film set had made me less of a believer. And with good reason.

I saw Vikrant entering the theater. I thought I might be imagining things.

What is he doing here? I wondered.

He had turned down my invitation to the premiere. Maybe he'd changed his mind at the last minute.

"Murat Khan!" voices shouted.

A group of fans suddenly rushed toward Murat while he was signing autographs.

"Move!" one of them said rudely to Vikrant, pushing him out of the way.

My fingernails dug into the palm of my hand. I found myself getting angry for some reason.

That is no way to treat a hero! I thought.

It was true that Vikrant had insisted on being anonymous. No one really knew this film was based on him. But shouldn't they at least consider that an ordinary-looking man could be a hero?

Vikrant didn't seem as bothered as I was.

He is always as cool as cucumber, I thought.

Our eyes locked. I felt my heart beat. What was happening to me?

The movie was about to start. Everyone was asked to take a seat.

I sat with the rest of the film's crew. The first two rows had been reserved for the A-listers, like Murat and his family, the director and producer, film critics, and socialites.

I scanned the crowd for Vikrant. I realized he was seated in the last row. The distance from the screen and the dim lights gave him the anonymity he liked.

Once again, our eyes met in the dark. I felt my heart skip a beat.

I thought, *Something is not right, Niyati!*

The film started. I saw my name on the screen, following the more important names.

This was it. This was my big moment.

Once the film started, I wondered why my thoughts kept drifting back to Vikrant. I kept hoping he was enjoying the dialogue I had written for his character. I turned my head to get a good look at him. I felt better.

He was smiling.

I smiled back, watching the rest of the movie in pieces. I was busy sneaking looks at Vikrant the entire time.

Finally, it was the big fire scene. I was over-joyed to see the reaction from the audience. They clapped, whistled, and cried when Murat fought the robbers and put out the fire.

"Murat! Murat! Murat!" they all cheered to-gether.

Except I didn't see Murat doing those stunts. I saw Vikrant.

He was helping a hundred people get out of the train. He was taking them safely to the hospital, risking his own life.

I was already getting goosebumps. I was so overwhelmed with emotions. Tears were starting in my eyes. The sentimental soundtrack did not help.

I turned to look back at Vikrant.

Except he wasn't there.

Where had he gone during the most important scene of the film?

I waited for a while before finally deciding to find him myself. It didn't take too long.

Vikrant was standing on the street just outside the theater. He turned toward me in surprise.

"You actually came," I said. I stood in front of

him with my heart beating like a fangirl's. "And you are already leaving?"

He shrugged. He pushed his sliding glasses back to the top of his nose.

"The fire scene just brought back so many memories. Of course, everything didn't happen in the same exciting way the film shows it," he said.

"I know. You lost Mochi that day," I said, "but people do need a happy ending."

He nodded. I noticed how his eyes sparkled with tears that never fell. He gave me a polite smile and started to leave.

"Vikrant, I—" I started to say.

I wanted to say something, anything to stop him. But words wouldn't come naturally to me in moments when I needed them the most. It was ironic, for a screenwriter.

"Yes?" he asked.

"I was wondering if you wanted a cup of coffee," I managed to say.

The silence was awkward. I wondered if I had crossed some sort of line.

"Sure," he said, smiling with his eyes. "I thought you would never ask."

I could finally think about the happiest moment of my life. It was the day of the film's premiere.

The day when I went out for coffee with a real-life hero.

About the Author

Rachita Ramya is a contributing author to the Storyshares library.

About the Publisher

Storyshares is a publisher focused on supporting the millions of teens and adults who struggle with reading by creating a new shelf in the library specifically for them. The ever-growing collection features content that is compelling and culturally relevant for teens and adults, yet still readable at a range of lower reading levels.

Storyshares generates content by engaging deeply with writers, bringing together a community to create this new kind of book. With more intriguing and approachable stories to choose from, the teens and adults who have fallen behind are improving their skills and beginning to discover the joy of reading.
For more information, visit storyshares.org.

Easy to Read. Hard to Put Down.

www.ingramcontent.com/pod-product-compliance
Lightning Source LLC
Chambersburg PA
CBHW071230170626
46809CB00005BA/2012